HORRiD HENRY
Reads a Book

HORRiD HENRY
Reads a Book

Francesca Simon
Illustrated by Tony Ross

Orion
Children's Books

Horrid Henry Reads a Book originally appeared in
Horrid Henry's Stinkbomb first published in Great Britain in 2002 by
Orion Children's Books
This edition first published in Great Britain in 2011
by Orion Children's Books
a division of the Orion Publishing Group Ltd
Orion House
5 Upper Saint Martin's Lane
London WC2H 9EA
An Hachette UK Company

1 3 5 7 9 10 8 6 4 2

The Orion Publishing Group's policy is to use papers that
are natural, renewable and recyclable products and made
from wood grown in sustainable forests. The logging and
manufacturing processes are expected to conform to the
environmental regulations of the country of origin.

A catalogue record for this book is available from the British Library.

ISBN 978 1 4440 0106 8

Printed and bound in China

www.orionbooks.co.uk
www.horridhenry.co.uk

For Josh

Look out for . . .

Don't Be Horrid, Henry!
Horrid Henry's Birthday Party
Horrid Henry's Holiday
Horrid Henry's Underpants
Horrid Henry Gets Rich Quick
Horrid Henry and the Football Fiend
Horrid Henry's Nits
Horrid Henry and Moody Margaret
Horrid Henry's Thank You Letter

There are many more
Horrid Henry books available.

You can find a complete list of backlist titles at
www.orionbooks.co.uk
or
www.horridhenry.co.uk

Contents

Chapter 1

Blah blah blah blah blah.

Miss Battle-Axe droned on
and on and on.

Horrid Henry drew pictures
of crocodiles tucking into a juicy
Battle-Axe snack in his maths book.

Snap!
Off went her head.

Yank!
Bye bye leg.

Crunch!
Ta-ta teeth.

Yum yum.

Henry's crocodile
had a big fat smile
on its face.

Blah blah blah
books
Blah blah blah
read
Blah blah blah
prize
Blah blah blah . . .
PRIZE?

Horrid Henry stopped doodling.
"What prize?" he shrieked.

"Don't shout out, Henry,"
said Miss Battle-Axe.

Horrid Henry waved his hand
and shouted: "What prize?"

"Well, Henry, if you'd been
paying attention instead of scribbling,
you'd know, wouldn't you?"
said Miss Battle-Axe.

Horrid Henry scowled.

Typical teacher.

You're interested enough
in what they're saying to ask
a question, and suddenly
they don't want to answer.

"So class, as I was saying before
I was so rudely interrupted . . ."
She glared at Horrid Henry.
"You'll have two weeks to read
as many books as you can for our
school reading competition.

Whoever reads the most books
will win an exciting prize.
A very exciting prize. But remember,
a book report on every book on
your list, please."

Oh. A reading competition.
Horrid Henry slumped in his chair.

Chapter 2

Phooey. Reading was hard, heavy work.

Just turning the pages made Henry feel exhausted.

Why couldn't they ever do
fun competitions,
like whose tummy could rumble
the loudest,

or who shouted out the most in class,

or who knew the rudest words?

Horrid Henry would win those
competitions every time.

But no.

Miss Battle-Axe would never
have a fun competition.
Well, no way was he taking part
in a reading contest.

Henry would just have to
watch someone undeserving like
Clever Clare or Brainy Brian
swagger off with the prize while
he sat prize-less at the back.

It was so unfair!

"What's the prize?" shouted
Moody Margaret.

Probably something awful like a
pencil case, thought Horrid Henry.
Or a bumper pack of school
tea towels.

"Sweets!"
shouted Greedy Graham.

"A million pounds!"
shouted Rude Ralph.

"Clothes!" shouted
Gorgeous Gurinder.

"A skateboard!"
shouted Aerobic Al.

"A hamster!"
said Anxious Andrew.

"Silence!" bellowed Miss Battle-Axe. "The prize is a family ticket to a brand new theme park."

Chapter 3

Horrid Henry sat up. A theme park!
Oh wow! He loved theme parks!
Rollercoasters! Water rides!
Candy floss!

His mean, horrible parents never
took him to theme parks.

They dragged him to museums.

They hauled him on hikes.

But if he won the competition,
they'd have to take him.

He had to win that prize.

He had to.

But how could he win
a reading competition without
reading any books?

"Do comics count?"
shouted Rude Ralph.

Horrid Henry's heart leapt.
He was king of the comic book
readers. He'd easily win a
comic book competition.

Miss Battle-Axe glared at Ralph
with her beady eyes.
"Of course not!" she said.
"Clare! How many books do you
think you can read?"

"Fifteen,"
said Clever Clare.

"Brian?"

"Eighteen,"
said Brainy Brian.

"Nineteen," said Clare.
"Twenty," said Brian.

Horrid Henry smiled.
Wouldn't they get a shock when
he won the prize? He'd start reading
the second he got home.

Chapter 4

Horrid Henry stretched out in the comfy black chair and switched on the TV. He had plenty of time to read. He'd start tomorrow.

Tuesday.

Oh boy! Five new comics!
He'd read them first and start
on all those books later.

Wednesday.

Whoopee! A *Mutant Max*
TV special! He'd definitely get
reading afterwards.

Thursday.

Rude Ralph brought round
his great new computer game,
Mash 'em! Smash 'em!
Henry mashed and smashed
and mashed and smashed…

Friday.

Yawn. Horrid Henry was exhausted after his long, hard week. I'll read tons of books tomorrow, thought Henry. After all, there was loads of time till the competition ended.

"How many books have *you* read,
Henry?" asked Perfect Peter,
looking up from the sofa.

"Loads," lied Henry.

"I've read five,"
said Perfect Peter proudly.
"More than anyone in my class."

"Goody for you," said Henry.

"You're just jealous,"
said Peter.

"As if I'd ever be jealous of you,
worm," sneered Henry.
He wandered over to the sofa.
"So what are you reading?"

"*The Happy Nappy*," said Peter.

The Happy Nappy! Trust Peter
to read a stupid book like that.

"What's it about?"
asked Henry, snorting.

"It's great," said Peter.
"It's all about this nappy . . ."

Then he stopped. "Wait, I'm not
telling *you*. You just want to find out
so you can use it in the competition.
Well, you're too late. Tomorrow is
the last day."

Horrid Henry felt as if a dagger
had been plunged into his heart.
This couldn't be.

Tomorrow!

How had tomorrow
sneaked up so fast?

"What!" shrieked Henry.
"The competition ends – tomorrow?"

"Yes," said Peter.
"You should have started reading
sooner. After all, why put off till
tomorrow what you can do today?"

"Shut up!" said Horrid Henry.
He looked around wildly.
What to do, what to do. He had
to read something, anything – fast.

"Gimme that!" snarled Henry,
snatching Peter's book.
Frantically, he started to read:

"I'm unhappy, pappy,"
said the snappy nappy.
"A happy nappy is a clappy . . ."

Perfect Peter snatched back his book.
"No!" screamed Peter, holding on
tightly. "It's mine!"

Henry lunged.

"Mine!"

"Mine!"

Riii–iippp.

"MUUUUMMMM!" screamed
Peter. "Henry tore my book!"

Mum and Dad ran into the room.

"You're fighting – over a book?"
said Mum. She sat down in a chair.

"I'm speechless," said Mum.

"Well, I'm not," said Dad. "Henry! Go to your room!"

"Fine!" screamed Horrid Henry.

Chapter 5

Horrid Henry prowled up
and down his bedroom.
He had to think of something. Fast.

Aha! The room was full of books.
He'd just copy down lots of titles.
Phew. Easy-peasy.

And then suddenly Horrid Henry remembered. He had to write a book report for every book he read.

Rats.

Miss Battle-Axe knew loads and
loads of books. She was sure to know
the plot of *Jack the Kangaroo* or
The Adventures of Terry the Tea Towel.

Well, he'd just have to borrow
Peter's list.

Horrid Henry sneaked into
Peter's bedroom. There was Peter's
competition entry, in the centre
of Peter's immaculate desk.

Henry read it.

Of course Peter would have
the boring and horrible
Mouse Goes to Town.

Could he live with the shame of having baby books like *The Happy Nappy* and *Mouse Goes to Town* on his competition entry?

For a day at a theme park, anything.

Quickly, Henry copied
Peter's list and book reports.

Whoopee! Now he had five books.
Wheel of Death here I come,
thought Horrid Henry.

Then Henry had to face the
terrible truth. Peter's books wouldn't
be enough to win. He'd heard
Clever Clare had seventeen.

If only he didn't have to write those
book reports. Why oh why did
Miss Battle-Axe have to know
every book ever written?

And then suddenly
Henry had a
brilliant, spectacular idea.

It was so brilliant, and so simple,
that Horrid Henry was amazed.

Of course there were books that
Miss Battle-Axe didn't know.
Books that hadn't been written – yet.

Horrid Henry grabbed his list.
"*Mouse Goes to Town*. The thrilling
adventures of a mouse in town.
He meets a dog, a cat, and a duck."

Why should that poor mouse
just go to town?
Quickly Henry began to scribble.

"*Mouse Goes to the Country*.
The thrilling adventures of a mouse
in the country. He meets . . ."
Henry paused. What sort of things
did you meet in the country?
Henry had no idea.
Aha. Henry wrote quickly.
"He meets a sheep and a werewolf."

"*Mouse Goes Round the World.*
Mouse discovers that the world
is round."

"*Mouse Goes to the Loo.*
The thrilling adventures of
one mouse and his potty."

Now, perhaps, something
a little different.

How about *A Boy and his Pig*.
What could that book be about?
thought Henry.
"Once upon a time there was a boy
and his pig. They played together
every day. The pig went oink."

Sounds good to me, thought Henry.

Then there was *A Pig and his Boy*.
And, of course, *A Boyish Pig*.
A Piggish Boy.

Two Pigs and a Boy.
Two Boys and a Pig.

Horrid Henry wrote and wrote
and wrote.

When he had filled up four pages
with books and reports,
and his hand ached from writing,
he stopped and counted…

Twenty-seven books!
Surely that was more than enough!

Chapter 6

Miss Battle-Axe rose from
her seat and walked to
the podium in the school hall.
Horrid Henry was so excited
he could scarcely breathe.
He had to win. He was sure to win.

"Well done, everyone," said Miss Battle-Axe. "So many wonderful books read. But sadly, there can only be one winner."

Me! thought Horrid Henry.

"The winner of the school reading competition, the winner who will be receiving a fabulous prize, is . . ."

Horrid Henry got ready to leap up.

"Clare, with twenty-eight books!"

Horrid Henry sank back down in his seat as Clever Clare swaggered up to the podium.

If only he'd added *Three Boys,
Two Pigs, and a Rhinoceros* to his list,
he'd have tied for first.

It was so unfair.

All his hard work for nothing.

"Well done, Clare!" beamed Miss Battle-Axe. She waved Clare's list. "I see you've read one of my favourites, *Boudicca's Big Battle*."

She stopped. "Oh dear. Clare, you've put down *Boudicca's Big Battle* twice by mistake. But never mind, I'm sure no one else has read *twenty-seven* books . . ."

"I have!" screamed Horrid Henry. Leaping and shouting, punching the air with his fist, Horrid Henry ran up onto the stage, chanting: "Theme park! Theme park! Theme park!"

"Gimme my prize!" he screeched,
snatching the tickets out of
Clare's hand.

"Mine!" screamed Clare,
snatching them back.

Miss Battle-Axe looked grim.
She scanned Henry's list.
"I am not familiar with the
Boy and Pig series," she said.

"That's 'cause it's Australian,"
said Horrid Henry.

Miss Battle-Axe glared at him.
Then she tried to twist her face
into a smile.

"It appears we have a tie," she said.
"Therefore, you will each receive a
family pass to the new theme park,
Book World. Congratulations."

Horrid Henry stopped his
victory dance.

Book World?
Book World?

Surely he'd heard wrong?

"Here are just some of the wonderful attractions you will enjoy at Book World," said Miss Battle-Axe.

"Thrill to a display of speed-reading!"

"Practise checking out library books!"

"Read to the beat!"

"Oh my, doesn't that sound fun!"

"AAAAAARGGGGGGGGG!"

screamed Horrid Henry.

HORRID HENRY BOOKS

Joke Books

Horrid Henry's Joke Book
Horrid Henry's Jolly Joke Book
Horrid Henry's Mighty Joke Book
Horrid Henry's Hilariously Horrid Joke Book

Early Readers

Don't be Horrid, Henry
Horrid Henry's Birthday Party
Horrid Henry's Holiday
Horrid Henry's Underpants
Horrid Henry Gets Rich Quick
Horrid Henry and the Football Fiend
Horrid Henry's Nits
Horrid Henry and Moody Margaret
Horrid Henry's Thank You Letter

Horrid Henry is also available on CD and as a digital download, all read by Miranda Richardson.